The Happy End Series

Stories from Barrow Magna

By
Paul Newnton

Stories from Barrow Magna

Author: Paul Newnton

Copyright © 2025 Paul Newnton

The right of Paul Newnton to be identified as author of this work has been asserted by the author in accordance with section 77 and 78 of the Copyright, Designs and Patents Act 1988.

ISBN 978-1-83538-529-6 (Paperback)
978-1-83538-562-3 (E-Book)

Book Cover Design and Book Layout by:
White Magic Studios
www.whitemagicstudios.co.uk

Published by:
Maple Publishers
Fairbourne Drive, Atterbury,
Milton Keynes,
MK10 9RG, UK
www.maplepublishers.com

A CIP catalogue record for this title is available from the British Library.

All rights reserved. No part of this book may be reproduced or translated by any form or by any means, electronic or mechanical, including photocopying, recording or by any information storage and retrieval system without written permission from the author.

The views expressed in this work are solely those of the author and do not reflect the opinions of Publishers, and the Publisher hereby disclaims any responsibility for them. This book should not be used as a substitute for the advice of a competent authority, admitted or authorized to advise on the subjects covered.

CONTENTS

A Labour of Love 4

Whatever Will Be, Will Be 11

Reflections 20

Colours of the Rainbow 24

All's Well That Ends Well 29

Vegetable Marrows 36

A Fish Out of Water 45

A Song of Love 51

Letters From a Son 57

Photo Finish 60

How Does Your Garden Grow 67

A Labour of Love

We were arranging flowers in St Stephens' church when Timothy Watkins, our Vicar, came in and greeted us.

"Thank you, ladies. Flowers do brighten up the church, although," he said wistfully, looking up at the bare walls and the vaulted ceiling, "If only we had a Michelangelo to paint murals, we could brighten up the walls as well."

That started me thinking.

"Why couldn't we paint a mural in the church?" I said to Debbie.

She paused pouring the tea. "You need special instruction and special materials."

I took the cup she offered. "I'm sure we could do it."

She gave a wry smile. "You're serious? Don't forget my fear of heights. I couldn't do it."

Debbie and I are totally unalike. You wouldn't think we were sisters. Debbie is short with grey hair and I'm tall, with auburn hair. We're both getting on a bit, retired from our jobs and living in Barrow Magna, and certainly for me, time hangs heavily on my hands as I've always been the active one. Debbie seems much more content.

I began to get enthusiastic. "Why don't we learn the techniques! It can't be too difficult."

Once I'd thought of it, coincidence seemed to take over. The Vicar's sister, Samantha, had just returned from a trip to Venice. She was giving a talk in the Church Hall on what she had seen, illustrated by photographs. We attended with most of the Sunday congregation.

Samantha spoke enthusiastically about the wonderful paintings and the painted churches she had seen, projecting pictures of them onto the screen.

I whispered to Debbie, "That's where we need to go."

"Where?" she whispered back.

"Venice, of course. Someone there is bound to be able to teach us."

"Shhh," a severe-looking woman sitting next to us turned and gave us a disapproving look.

Afterwards, I had a word with Samantha who gave us the name of the travel agent she had used and the hotel where she had stayed.

I made all the arrangements, and apart from a very early start from Gatwick Airport, all went well. I enjoy flying. Debbie isn't so keen, but I thought she coped well. We arrived at Venice Marco Polo Airport where, although neither of us could speak the language, a helpful porter carried our suitcases, took us to a water taxi and saw us safely aboard.

The ride to our hotel was thrilling. The weather was gorgeous. The boat cut through the blue water, throwing up swathes of foam. Our driver shouted greetings to the boats that were passing us as we headed past pillars of wood marking our path. We passed small islands and then on to the waterfront of the Grand Canal where we landed close to a tangle of gondolas, the tall buildings looming over us.

A porter came out of the hotel we were to stay at and took our luggage. The woman at the reception welcomed us in English with a slight accent. She checked us into our rooms, and the porter showed us up.

We explored our bedrooms. Mine was huge, the wallpaper swirled with flower designs, and the bed was enormous, decorated with what looked like gold leaf. I bounced up and down on it as Debbie knocked and came in.

"It's like a palace," she said. "Our bedrooms are large enough to hold a ball in." She twirled around in joy.

I didn't want to lose any time, so after settling in, we went down to the concierge who was most helpful, directing us to the Comunità di artisti where he said we would find a community of painters who might help us.

It was strange walking out along the Grand Canal among crowds of tourists. Some of them were in groups headed by tour guides, holding an umbrella in the air.

The Comunità di artisti was a bit difficult to find as so many small lanes led off the main street, but we found it a little way from St Mark's Square.

It was an old building with quite a narrow entrance, but inside, the decorations were magnificent.

As we stood admiring them, a man came down the stairs and said something in Italian that I didn't understand, but it seemed like a question, so I said, "Do you speak English?"

The immediate reply was, "Of course. How can I help you Signorinas?"

Once Enrico Boskoni got over the shock of two very English ladies asking if someone would teach them to paint a religious mural on a church wall, he drew himself up to his full height and said, "Signorinas, I, Enrico, will teach you how to paint the beautiful scenes that you desire."

He took us to his studio on the first floor where he showed us examples of different types of murals, some religious, some more abstract.

"There is a difference between fresco painting and mural painting," he said. "Fresco painting is done with the paint incorporated into the plaster. That is the proper way, but I think you want to paint a mural on a wall that is already there?"

I looked at Debbie, "Yes, that is what we want."

"Then you shall have it," he said.

His fees were reasonable, but he was a hard taskmaster. He was restoring a painting of the twelve apostles in the Church of Saint Feligi, and he took us as his assistants along with a young Spaniard called Fernando. Before he would let us anywhere near the restoration, he made us practice painting on boards set up in his studio every day. He taught us the basic techniques, and only when he was satisfied did he let us go to the church.

While we were learning, we spent our free time exploring, going for a ride in a gondola down the Grand Canal to the Bridge of Sighs, drinking coffee at Florian's in St Mark's Square and exploring the vastness of the Basilica. It was an exciting time.

In the church, Enrico had erected a scaffolding up to the full-length painting with two platforms at different levels. When he learnt of Debbie's fear of heights, he arranged for her to work on the lower platform. He helped us mix the paints, explained what he wanted and then seemed to let us get on with it. In reality, I'm sure he kept a close eye on what we were doing, but he seemed pleased with the way the work was progressing.

"You have real talent," he said to us at one of our regular morning meetings.

He was a fat, jolly man, and I wondered how he managed to climb the ladder to the platform so nimbly like an Italian mountain goat. In fact, he was so agile and so fat, I could tell that Debbie had forgotten her fear of heights as she watched him climb.

One day after work, Fernando, the other assistant, suggested that we might like to join him for a meal. We got to know Fernando well, sharing a platform and painting with him, so we accepted gratefully.

The Grand Canal looked beautiful as we walked along it, the late sun beaming down on the glistening water.

"It's here," Fernando turned into a narrow lane.

He led the way into the café where the proprietor obviously knew him. He ushered us to a table at the back.

I gazed at the walls, which were full of religious paintings.

Fernando caught my gaze and said, "In the past, many famous painters have come here."

The proprietor beamed, "Yes, it is said that Michelangelo himself came in the sixteenth century. We have one of his paintings. See," he pointed to a particularly fine painting of the Madonna and Child.

Fernando was a good host, and the meal was excellent. By the end of the meal, I think I must have drunk a little too much wine, I needed to go to the toilet.

I spent some time combing my hair and making myself presentable. When it was time to go back, I was confused. The toilet had two doors, and I went through the wrong one.

It led into a narrow alley. I turned to what I thought was the front of the building but got lost in a maze of lanes.

"Excuse, Signorina, can I help?"

While I was looking around helplessly, an old man with a white beard had come up behind me. He was dressed in old-fashioned clothes.

"You speak English," I said.

"Yes, very well. I spent some years in England in the early days. My name is Michelangelo."

I was so confused, the name didn't register with me until later.

"I'm Linda Newnham, and I'm lost," I said. "Can you help me find the…"

I then realised I didn't know the name of the café. "I know it is a haunt of painters," I said.

"Don't worry, I know the place. I have been there many times," he smiled reassuringly.

He guided me back to the Grand Canal, and while we were walking, I told him where we were from and what we were doing. It was then that he talked about the painting of the Sistine Chapel, and I started to realise who he might be.

Before I could ask more questions, he pointed down the lane and said, "You will find your café along here."

Debbie and Fernando were standing outside. I rushed up to them.

"Did I give you a fright?" I said breathlessly.

"You certainly did. Where have you been?"

"I got lost but this man rescued me and led me back." I turned to thank him.

Fernando looked surprised. "There's no one here."

I suddenly had a strange creepy feeling. "He said his name was Michelangelo, and we talked about the Sistine Chapel. He was interested in what we wanted to do."

Debbie looked at me strangely. "You must have been dreaming. Michelangelo died in 1564, so he certainly wouldn't be around helping old ladies who got lost."

"That's spooky," Fernando shivered. "I think I should be getting you back to your hotel."

The work with Enrico went well, and both of us learnt a lot.

We came back to Barrow Magna and after submitting possible designs to the Parochial Church Council and reassuring them about our newfound skills, backed up by a testimonial from Enrico, we started painting a mural of the twelve apostles.

We were almost finished, and we stood looking up at the picture when we became aware of a bearded figure standing behind us.

"It is a fine painting, Signorinas."

I turned around. "It's you," I said with a shock of recognition.

"Who?" asked Debbie.

"Michelangelo, of course!" I grasped his hand. "I knew you were real, but what are you doing here?"

"I wanted to visit England again, so I thought I would come to see if you really had done what you said." He looked up at our painting, "and you have."

"Look here," Debbie said. "You told my sister you were Michelangelo. You can't be. He died centuries ago."

"But I am," Michelangelo laughed. "Not the famous artist, though. My mother named me after him, but I am a painter and have brought you a gift."

He lifted a covered package and gave it to me. "It is a painting of the Madonna and Child. Perhaps you would like to hang it in your church."

"Thank you," Debbie was so excited, she took it out of my hands, carefully peeling back the covering. As the painting was exposed, she exclaimed, "But she has only got one eye!"

Michelangelo laughed. "Of course, I studied under Pablo Picasso, I am a Cubist painter."

Now, when the Reverend Timothy Watkins shows visitors around his church, he proudly tells the story of how we went to Venice to learn the skills that led us to paint the mural. He also tells them that the church has a genuine Michelangelo, the latter, and if they ask to see it, he takes them to the darkest part of the church where the painting is kept.

Whatever Will Be, Will Be

It had been a hot summer's day. The two children sat in the long grass on Barrow Hill, making a daisy chain. They could feel the warmth of the sun and hear the birds chattering around them. Completely immersed in their own world, Selina and Linda had been happy.

As Selina thought back to those days, she remembered how carefree both had been. Selina had recently lost her husband after nursing him through a long illness. Her loss made her think about the meaning of life. In particular, it focussed her thoughts on the childhood friendship she had enjoyed with Linda.

They had kept in touch for years and years while Linda went to university and Selina, always the quiet one, trained as a nurse.

At first, they managed to take holidays together, and it was on one of these holidays in the South of France that Linda met Nigel, who was on his own for a walking holiday. Selina remembered the instant attraction between them. She had felt like an intruder and suggested she should go home and leave the two of them together, but Linda wouldn't hear of it. Thinking back, Selina thought Linda must have wanted her as a chaperone.

Linda and Nigel married. He was an architect, and it seemed that he spent his holidays going to interesting architectural sites and writing them up with photographs and plans for leading architecture magazines. He said this helped his career and got his name noticed. He was very successful.

Because they had met in the South of France, they purchased a rundown farmhouse in a village in the Languedoc, Nigel applying his skills, transforming it using local materials and artefacts. They lived in the farmhouse for part of the summer and rented it out through an agency for the rest of the year.

Selina was always welcome in both homes, one in Surrey and the other in France. They had often suggested that she go to their French home when they were not using it, but she had always resisted the idea. It would have made her feel lonely. That is until she met and married Eric. Eric was a military man, spending long periods abroad, so she became used to the solitary life. Now that he was gone, she realised that even when he wasn't with her, he had been a calming influence on her, a rock on which to build.

Denise and Frank, Selina's two children, had left home. Denise was married to a local builder, and Frank was pursuing studies at Brookshire University. Linda and Nigel had no children. They seemed to live a gay bohemian life in contrast to Selina's quiet one in Barrow Magna.

She and Linda had drifted apart in recent years, Linda with her high life and Selina nursing her sick husband. Now, they were both free. Linda by divorce and Selina, sadly freed by death, and Selina didn't like it.

Her first thought was to contact Linda. Apart from Christmas cards, there had been no real contact for years, but she knew that Linda still lived at the Surrey address. In the divorce settlement, she retained the house she and Nigel had lived in. Selina supposed Nigel would have kept the Languedoc house as he had lavished so much of his work and skills on it.

Her second thought was that Linda had her own life to lead, and there was no way they could go back to the closeness they had felt as children.

In the end, she sent Linda a long letter telling her of Eric's death and that the children had moved away. She didn't mention that she longed to see her again.

There was no reply to her letter, not in the first or the second week. Perhaps Linda wanted nothing more to do with her, or perhaps she was ill. She waited until the third week, and when there was still no reply to her letter, she decided she would wait no longer. She must act, but what could she do?

It was then that the idea came to her. She would go down to Surrey unannounced to see Linda. They would meet, be reunited, and things would be as they used to be.

She planned the journey. Train from Kemble to London Paddington, underground to Waterloo, train from there to Guildford. Taxi to Linda's house.

Fortunately, she had Paula Bentham as a neighbour who promised to keep an eye on the house for her. She gave Linda's address to Paula in case she needed to contact her. Then she set off, having ordered Jack Bolton's taxi to take her to the station.

It was quite a while since she had been on a train, but all went well. The train from Kemble was on time. The only trouble was, as soon as she was comfortably seated on the train, she began to worry. Had she locked the back door? Had she switched the stove off? She made a mental note to ring Paula as soon as she got to her destination and ask her to check. Selina was a chronic worrier, but when she got off the train at Paddington, she found plenty to occupy her mind.

Although Paddington station was unfamiliar to her, she found the steps leading to the underground easily. Round on the Circle line to Embankment, then one stop on the Northern line, and she was at Waterloo and going up the escalator towards the main station. As she stood among the press of people travelling in both directions, her gaze fell on a familiar-looking figure going past on the down escalator. It was Linda. Admittedly, a slightly older-looking Linda, but it was almost certainly her.

She reached the top of the escalator and started off down after her friend, who was about to go through the ticket barrier. She caught up, put a hand on her shoulder, and was shattered when the person turned round. It wasn't Linda. She apologised and quickly backed away.

A feeling of absolute despair came over her. She was about to resume her journey on the up escalator when a hand fell on her shoulder. This time it was Linda.

"What are you doing here?" Linda asked.

"Coming to see you," said Selina. "What are you doing?"

"Coming to see you," said Linda, laughing. "Let's go and have a coffee in the station buffet."

Seated at a table, they took stock of each other. Both looked a little older, as indeed they might, but both looked well.

"I received your letter, but you didn't put your address on it," said Linda. "Of course, I knew you were still in Barrow Magna, but I had lost my address book. I didn't know how to make contact, so I thought the best thing to do was to come and see you."

"I was doing the same," said Selina.

"Well, now that we have met, we have a lot of catching up to do."

It was a hot summer's day. Linda and Selina sat in the long grass on Barrow Hill, making a daisy chain. They could feel the warmth of the sun and hear the birds chattering around them. Completely immersed in their own world, they were happy. However, when they had done this as children, they didn't worry where they were sitting. Now, grownup, Selina worried about the damp grass and had spread a waterproof ground sheet for them to sit on.

Linda discovered that Selina was a chronic worrier. Even as they headed for Barrow Hill, Selina was worrying that she hadn't locked the back door, hadn't switched the stove off, and would the picnic they were taking be enough for them?

"Stop worrying and let whatever will be, will be," Linda advised, and to be fair to Selina, she did.

"It's so nice to have you here," she said. "I feel as though a weight has been taken off my shoulders."

"What weight is that?" asked Linda.

"Oh, you know. There seem so many things to worry about, and a trouble shared is a trouble halved."

Selina completed the daisy chain and hung it around Linda's neck.

"I wish we could be the carefree children we once were," she said.

"We can't be children again, but we can be happy," said Linda.

"What is happiness?" asked Selina. "I am happier now that you are here, but …"

That 'but' bothered Linda, and she set out to try to help her friend.

She found a list of evening courses that were being held in Barrow Magna.

"I would like to go to a lot of these," she said. "Here's one in Barrow Magna in Elizabethan Times. Ah, here's a coincidence! A course that should interest you. Don't worry, let whatever will be, will be. You ought to go to that."

"A course isn't going to stop me worrying," said Selina. "I just can't help it. It's the way I'm made, I suppose."

"Well, if you won't go for you, go for me," said Linda. "I'll come with you if you like."

They both enrolled and turned up on Wednesday evening for the first session held in Templeton Hall.

The tutor was Monica Brathwaite from Gloucester, where she ran a counselling service.

Six people turned up for the session. Besides Linda and Selina, there were four others, Jenny Milton, Elsie Owen, Tom Forester and Amelia Cranston. Five women and only one man.

Perhaps women worry more than men, thought Linda. I wonder what these people have to worry about! She soon found out, as Monica's method was to have them sit in a circle and get each person to give a five-minute talk about their worries and fears.

Amelia, Head Teacher at Barrow Magna's school, was probably the most articulate of the group as she was used to standing in front of people and talking. She gave the first talk.

"I have two main worries," she said. "First, I worry about all the children in my school. Are they making progress? Could we do better? Secondly, I worry about the reactions I sometimes get from the parents. We do get praise, but it only takes one bad criticism to upset me. How can I stop worrying about these things?"

Next was the farmer, Tom Forester. He was a good-natured, direct sort of person obviously in tune with the soil, and what he said surprised Linda.

"Farming isn't what it used to be. I worry all the time about the weather and my crops. Will it be a good harvest, or will the weather totally wreck the yield. I worry about the price I will get for my wheat. Sometimes, the price you get at the market isn't worth all the work you put into the sowing and the growing."

Monica was making notes as they talked. Now, it was Selina's turn.

"I'm not used to speaking in public," she said. "In any case, my worries are trivial compared to the other two."

Monica looked across at her. "Don't worry about it. Perhaps you can tell us later when we get more into the course. Linda, would you like to speak about your worries?"

"I'm a bit of a fraud in this course," she said. "I came along to support Selina, but yes, I do have one worry. What happens when we die?"

"That's exactly one of my worries," said Jenny. "Is there another world? Do we go there when we die, or is it just oblivion? Does God exist? All sorts of questions like that."

"That's a difficult one," said Monica, "We shall have to come back to that. Elsie, you haven't said anything yet. Tell us about your worries."

"Mine are of a business nature," Elsie said. "I run the toyshop in Cirencester. Fashions keep changing. I always worry I shall end up with a lot of unsold stock, which would affect my cash flow."

Monica turned to all of them, "You have to remember," she said, "that yesterday is gone, and tomorrow is yet to come. Today is where you are living now. Nothing you can do will alter what you did yesterday, and although you can plan for the future, you don't need to worry about it, as whatever will be, will be. Most of your worries are future things, and in this course, we shall be looking at how you can handle them."

She talked about the difference between worry and proper concern, outlining the effect worry could have on their emotions, their nervous system and their health. The session ended with her asking everyone to analyse their worries and try to bring to the class next week at least one possible solution to them. She also asked Selina to prepare a five-minute talk and present it at the next session.

"And don't worry about it all week," she said.

As they were going out, Tom Forrester said to Amelia, "I don't see how I can find a solution to my problems."

"I know mine are affecting my health," said Amelia, "but well, see you next week."

Next week's session seemed to come quickly. They all assembled in Templeton Hall, all except Jenny.

"Jenny sent her apologies," said Monica. "She had to go visit her mother who is ill. Let's begin with Selina's talk."

Selina had rehearsed what she was going to say several times, but she still felt nervous. She described how she worried about everything.

Monica pointed out that Selina's worries were common to many people and were caused very often by lapses of memory. She went on to ask the others if they had been able to find a solution to their worries.

"I have," said Elsie. "You remember I was worried I would end up with a lot of unsold stock, which would affect my cash flow. I talked it over with my husband and he pointed out that the real problem was how to get rid of the unsold stock. I then realised something I should have thought of a long time ago, and that was to only accept stock on a sale or return basis."

"Tom, what about you?" Monica asked.

"No," he said. "I don't think my problems have a solution. Not one I can think of anyway."

"All problems have a solution," said Monica. "Even if the answer is to do nothing."

"But what can I do about the weather and my crops? How do I know if it will be a good harvest or if the weather will totally wreck the yield? Then there is the worry about the price I will get for my wheat."

"Let's consider your case," said Monica. "Obviously, you can't influence the weather. How long have you been farming now?"

"Twenty-five years," said Tom.

"In those twenty-five years, how many times have your crops failed?"

Tom scratched his head. "Now, I recall only once, and I was able to salvage something out of that."

"So, the chance that it will happen again is one in twenty-five. Quite long odds."

"I see what you mean when you put it like that," said Tom.

"One standard way of avoiding worry is with what I call the three-step formula. You might all benefit from this one. Here's the formula:

Whatever you are worrying about, what is the worst thing that can happen?

Be prepared to accept this. This should quiet your mind so that you can go to the third step, which is:

Think about possible ways to overcome the problem."

After the course, Selina was quite pleased with the way she had given her talk and was reassured that many other people had the same problems.

"I think the three-step method Monica suggested is quite useful," she said. "The worst thing that can happen if I leave the stove on when I go out is that it will either burn out or just go on heating. If it burns out, I get it repaired, and if it goes on heating, there wouldn't be anything on it to catch fire, so I don't need to worry about it. That made me realise what I can do about it."

"What's that?" asked Linda.

"Make a list of things to check before I go out. That way, I can remove my worries and go out without worries on my mind."

On the course, Linda and Selina learnt several other ways to defeat worry, including keeping busy, giving yourself no time for worry, living for today and not worrying about the past or excessively about the future. Monica told them how they could review the events of the day, such as writing a diary, making a note of things they weren't happy with and resolving to do them better next time.

"Getting things on paper often gets things off your mind," she said.

Amelia thought this advice would be particularly useful for her as she already kept a school log. She could extend this to a private diary where she recorded her thoughts and actions.

The next day, Linda and Selina went up onto Barrow Hill. It was a hot summer's day, and they sat in the long grass making a daisy chain. They could feel the warmth of the sun and hear the birds chattering around them. Completely immersed in their own world, they were both happy, and Selina was totally relaxed.

Reflections

The water sparkled in the sun. Small, fluffy clouds hung suspended in the clear blue sky. I'm sitting on a bench, holding my notebook and facing a placid lake where ducks are swimming nearby around the edges of the water lilies.

Lindle Manor, just outside Barrow Magna and near Cirencester, is the ideal writer's retreat. I'm giving myself time to think and to write.

I've written stories since I was a teenager. Not many were published, but once writing gets into your blood, you can't stop. Words on paper are my way of sorting things out. We had been given our first assignment to go out into the grounds of the Manor and write on any subject we liked, but for once, the words won't come. It's my first day and I'm so bound up with my thoughts that everything seems a jumble.

Perhaps that's it. Write about a couple who don't talk to each other anymore, that's why I'm here. Ideas begin to flow. As I'm writing, an inquisitive duck comes up and looks at me hopefully.

I shake my head. "Sorry, duck. I don't have anything for you."

It looks disappointed and turns away, searching among the lily pads.

I go back into the house. It's rather grand, a pillared entrance leading into a spacious hall, bedrooms up a grand staircase on the left. Lounge and dining room on the right.

There are five of us on the retreat. I'm Ann Aplet, then there's a couple, Sam and Josy Carter, and two other rather timid women, I don't know their names yet. Our host is Evelyn Jackson, a well-known author. She owns Lindle Manor.

Dinner was a subdued affair. The grand dining room lit by flickering candles seemed to make everything sombre and dark. Shadows wavered spreading up into the vaulted ceiling. No one talked much. Everyone seemed to be summing each other up. I felt uncomfortable.

After dinner, we went to a comfortable lounge, brightly lit with chairs grouped around a cheerful log fire, which I'm sure made everyone feel better. I know it did me, although I still felt nervous.

I was heartened to find that most members of the group found their assignment difficult, and it was obvious that Josy and Sam were in the middle of a grand row. The looks they gave each other and their body language showed clearly how they felt about each other, and what they had written reflected their antagonism. Then it was my turn to read.

"I'm sorry," I said, "but I seem to be suffering from writer's block. The few words I've written aren't worth reading out loud."

Evelyn looked at me sympathetically. She was slim and elderly. "Don't worry," she said. "It can take a little time to relax and tune in."

Later, she stood up to make an announcement.

"People come here to write, but you can use this just as a retreat, or you can follow the writing assignments that I lay out for you. Either way, my staff and I will try to make this a place where you can relax and forget your troubles for a while."

Next morning, I was late coming downstairs. The others must have had breakfast already. As I sat alone, Evelyn came across to me.

"You're troubled," she said. "You are here for a reason not connected with writing?"

"You're right," I said, "I love writing, but this is personal. I don't want to discuss it at the moment."

Evelyn got up. "Take your time," she said. "Enjoy a walk."

I took her advice and went down towards the lake. As I walked through the woods, I could hear voices. It was Josy and Sam Carter. I didn't mean to eavesdrop, but they were talking so loudly I couldn't help hearing what was said.

"We're not the same together, and I don't know why," Josy said.

"We've gone over this time and time again," Sam raised his voice.

"You don't understand," Josy said in a tearful voice.

"Of course I understand," he said loudly. "You think I'm neglecting you for my work. Well, let me tell you, without this job, I wouldn't be able to keep you in the manner you would expect."

I should have walked on, but I stood behind a tree, listening as it was so like my own situation. Suddenly, there was a rustle, and Josy almost cannoned into me. She was crying.

"Oh," she said, "It's you." She ran off blindly in the direction of the house. I walked on and came across Sam sitting on a bench in the middle of a clearing in the woods. He sat huddled, head down, shoulders hunched. I was tempted to sit and try to comfort him, he looked so forlorn, but I left him and went back to my seat near the ducks.

Now I knew what I wanted to write about. Josy and Sam's arguments echoed exactly the silly arguments I have been having with Rob. I wrote rapidly, pouring my heart out to Rob on paper, then I took out my mobile phone and texted him. "I miss you."

After dinner, I read out what I had written to the others. I could see Josy and Sam looking at each other as I read. Josy had a tear in her eye, Sam looked thoughtful.

Afterwards, Evelyn stopped me as I went up the stairs.

"You're looking happier," she said.

"I am," I said. "Thinking about someone else's problems helped."

Next morning, Josy and Sam came in for breakfast holding hands, looking more relaxed.

Evelyn stood up, coffee cup in hand, "Your next assignment is to write about something you would do differently. Until lunchtime, you are free to write, walk, do just as you please."

I went back to my room. My phone beeped. It was a text.

"I'm on my way. Love Rob."

I took my notepad down to the lake. This time the words began to flow. I knew what I would do differently.

I put down my pad and sat watching a gorgeous peacock butterfly fluttering over the lake. So beautiful, giving pleasure with its brilliant colours, but so short a life. Life was short, and now, I must live it to the full. I realised that you can't retreat from life and that I loved Rob dearly.

I bent over, looking at my reflection in the water, and as I did so, a hand touched my shoulder. Rob's reflection appeared by my side.

Colours of the Rainbow

It was a glorious day in Barrow Magna. They were setting up the Annual Fair on the green. The decorative caravans were parked at the edge of the green, and in the middle, tents were being pegged, stalls were being erected. There was much hammering and activity. The fair on the green was traditional. Once a year, Rose Turner brought Turner's Amusements to Barrow Magna to set up dodgems, a carousel, various rides and stalls. These were mixed with local stalls, bring and buy, and local crafts.

Cara was a teacher at the local school across the green, and her best friend Lucy was also a teacher at the same school.

During the lunch break that Friday, Lucy asked if Cara was going to the fair. "I'm going with my boyfriend, Glen," she said.

"Yes, Shaun has asked me. Why don't we make it a foursome?" This was unusual for Cara, as it was usually Lucy who took the initiative.

Lucy was a short, fiery redhead, full of energy and practical to the extreme, whereas Cara was the exact opposite, tall, blonde, willowy and full of romantic notions.

Cara's boyfriend, Shaun, worked in the estate agents in the nearby town, and although they had been going out together for almost a year, Cara wasn't sure if he was serious about her.

Getting ready for the fair, Cara pulled on her latest pair of vivid pink, wide-bottomed trousers. She looked at herself in the mirror. She felt comfortable in them with the lacy long-sleeved blouse that complemented her outfit.

Humming "Love, love me do, you know I love you, I'll always be true," she did a little dance round the room.

"Shaun's here," her mother, Mona, called up to her.

"I'll be there in a minute."

She sat at the dressing table, combing her long blonde hair and twisting it back into a ponytail. "No," she let the hair fall over her eyes. "Shaun likes it loose, but do I like Shaun enough to settle down with him?" she swept it back from her face. A last look in the mirror, then she raised her left hand and looked intently at her third finger.

"Love me, love me do," she said softly under her breath.

She looked over the banister at Shaun as she came down the stairs.

"You look great," he said, kissing her on the cheek as she reached the bottom.

Cara gave a little twirl. "Thank you, kind sir."

"Have a good time at the fair," her mother smiled at them.

"Mum, why don't you and Dad come?" she asked, as she held Shaun's hand.

"Fairs are for young people," said Dylan, her father, coming in from the garden.

He clasped his wife, Mona around the waist and looked at her lovingly. "We met at the fair all those years ago, and it was love at first sight. Do you remember?"

"How could I forget!" she squeezed his hand. "I was so scared on the roller coaster that I grabbed the person next to me, and it was you. We went for an ice cream and although I had come with my sister, we spent the rest of the day together." She looked at him with love in her eyes.

I wish Shaun would look at me like that, but he doesn't, Cara thought, as she tugged him to the door. She turned and looked back at her parents who were still hugging each other. *I'm so lucky to have them*, she thought. *Could Shaun and I be like that?*

Mona gave Cara a knowing look. "Be off with you," she said, hugging closer to Dylan.

It was a lovely sunny day, the air was full of the sound of the fair, the busy chatter of voices, children calling, and you could feel the excitement. The green was packed with people eating ice cream, crowding around the various stalls, riding on the dodgems and children riding on the merry-go-round that was churning out all the old tunes.

"There's Lucy and Glen," said Cara, "I promised we would meet up with them. Come on." She dragged Shaun over. "Should we go around together or just split up and meet back later?" she asked Lucy.

"I promised Glen a ride on the dodgems," said Lucy. "You go on, we can meet up later."

"Right, come on Shaun, let's have our fortune told."

"Must we," he said. "I wanted to go on the dodgems."

"Don't be a spoilsport, here's the fortune teller's tent, let's go in."

Rose Turner always played the part of the fortune teller. She sat behind a small table covered with a gold-coloured cloth. A crystal ball reflected the light from the spotlight above her head. Her heavy bangles and beads jangled as she greeted them.

"Hullo my dear," she said to Cara. "Come to have your fortune told?" She took a shrewd look at Shaun who was embarrassed and was trying to hang back.

"I won't bite, come and sit down, both of you."

They sat in front of her. Rose gazed into her crystal.

"I see the two of you at the fair. One of you has a secret. I can't tell what it is. Let me see your hand."

She reached over, and to Shaun's surprise, took his hand. He moved as if to jerk it away, but she held on firmly. She turned it over and studied his palm. "Now, you," she took Cara's smaller hand and looked at them together.

She looked serious for a moment, "I see a car crash, but then you will find happiness at the end of the rainbow." She released their hands.

"What does it mean?" asked Cara, holding Shaun's hand nervously. "Will we be all right?"

Rose got up from her chair. "I can tell you no more," she said. "You must face your destiny together."

Shaun put some coins in her hand and dragged Cara out of the tent.

Rose looked on with a smile on her face. *A lovely young couple, he's too shy to ask her, but perhaps, well, we shall see.*

Outside the tent, Shaun shook his head and said, "What a load of rubbish. Let's have a go at the rifle range."

"You know I don't like guns. Must we?" she asked.

"I want to win something for you. Come on."

"Three shots in the bullseye, and you win a prize," shouted the old man behind the counter, handing Shaun a rifle.

Shaun took aim and put two out of three shots in the bullseye.

"Hard luck, young man. Trying to win a cuddly toy for your young lady? Have another go."

So, Shaun did, and this time, put three shots in the centre of the target.

The man smiled and handed Cara a floppy rabbit. "Nice young man you've got there."

Cara dangled the rabbit by one ear. "I know," she said smiling at the man.

"What's next?" she asked Shaun.

"Let's go on the dodgems." He looked up at the sky. "It looks like rain. Let's get under cover."

Cara climbed into one car while Shaun climbed into another. He lost sight of her until suddenly there was a crash as a car bumped into him. It was Cara.

"She said we should have a crash," she yelled at him over the noise of the music and screams as more people bumped into each other. She waved her rabbit, "So, that was it?"

"There's Lucy and Glen," she waved as they headed towards them, and their four cars bumped.

"Now we've all had a car crash," Cara laughed. Glen and Lucy looked puzzled. When they got off the dodgems, Cara explained. "The gypsy told us we should have a car crash, but we would find happiness at the end of the rainbow."

"That means a crock of gold," Lucy said, "You find a crock of gold at the end of the rainbow."

"You don't believe that, do you?" Glen said.

"I'm not sure," Cara looked at Shaun. "Shaun, what do you think?"

"I think we are going to get wet," he looked up at the gathering clouds.

Lucy whispered to Glen, "I think Shaun has got something he wants to say to Cara. Let's go and leave them alone."

"OK," Glen took her by the hand. "Well, goodbye, you two. Hope you find your rainbow." They disappeared into the crowd.

"I wanted us to be alone," Shaun said, "Let's sit the next one out."

He led the way to a bench at the edge of the green.

They sat down, and Shaun was about to say something when the heavens opened, and a torrent of rain poured down on them. Shaun quickly took off his jacket and put it over Cara's shoulders.

The rain stopped as quickly as it had started, the sun came out and a gorgeous rainbow appeared, hovering over their heads.

"There's the rainbow, but where's the crock of gold?" Cara asked, her face lit by the wonderful colours.

"You're my crock of gold," Shaun said, kneeling carefully on the wet ground. "Will you marry me?"

Cara, bathed in the light of the rainbow, pulled him to his feet, "Of course, I will, you daft thing, but now let's go home and get dry."

All's Well That Ends Well

"I can't abide strong drink," Annalicia confided to Penny Winsom who lived in the cottage next to hers, down at Diggers Bottom.

Annalicia Pending was not really against alcohol but was afraid that if she took a drink, her tongue would run away with her, and she would confess her secret to everyone.

Her secret was simple, she was incapable of making decisions but knew she mustn't show it. To everyone else in the village of Barrow Magna, she was a pillar of strength, someone they could take their troubles to, and most times, she would help either with wise words or actions.

She looked comfortable with herself, her large, twinkling blue eyes seemed to see beyond the thing she was looking at, and she always had a smile on her lips.

Barrow Magna is a small village in the Cotswolds. It has a village store and post office, a church, St Stephens, a village hall, two pubs and a school.

Annalicia was into everything in the village, but at the end of every day, she would sink into the rocking chair by her Aga stove and thank God for letting her get through the day without showing how scared she was at making a wrong decision.

Her method for overcoming this problem was to listen carefully to what someone had to say, then, if there was a choice between two courses of action, she would pick one at random. So far, it had always worked, but it left her nerves on a knife-edge in case, one day, it didn't work.

She had this problem all her life, but through long practice, she had developed her method of deciding to such a fine art that no one in the village had the slightest idea of the agonies she went through.

In fact, no one in the village could remember a time when Annalicia had not been there to help them. She was an institution like the village shop.

Every morning, she went to the shop to get her newspaper and the groceries she needed.

One morning, Fred Jackson was already in the shop buying some cheese as she walked in.

"Morning Fred," she said as the girl behind the counter handed her the newspaper without her asking.

"You don't look very happy," she looked at his dismal face.

Fred put the cheese down on the counter. "What is there to be happy about?" he said.

"That doesn't sound like you, Fred."

"Well, since I've retired and the missus has gone, life don't seem worth living."

"You used to work on the railway, didn't you, Fred?"

"Yes," he said proudly, lifting his shoulders, "Man and boy, I miss it! Out in all weathers, but it ain't done me any harm."

Annalicia paid for her papers and groceries, said goodbye to Fred and walked out of the shop looking thoughtfully.

When she had put her groceries away, instead of settling down to read the paper before it was time for elevenses, she walked over to talk to Penny Winsom.

Penny was in her front garden, hoeing weeds in the flower beds.

"Hello, Anna. You're around early. Want a cup of coffee? I'm about ready for one, come on in."

Penny's house was neat as a pin. Annalicia looked around at the polished table, the bowl of flowers adding a golden glow to the surface and the carefully placed cushions on the comfortable sofa as Penny motioned her to sit down.

"I'll just get the coffee," Penny said. "It's already brewing."

Annalicia got up and walked over to the mantelpiece, looking at the photograph of Penny and her husband. She turned as Penny came in bearing a tray, which she set down on the table, moving the flowers to one side.

"He was a fine-looking man, your husband," she said, taking her seat on the sofa again.

Penny sighed, "Yes, I do miss him, but at least volunteering in the shop has helped me make new friends and, of course, with you next door as a good neighbour." She poured the coffee. "You like it without milk, don't you?"

Annalicia took the cup, "Yes, thanks. I wanted to talk to you about volunteering," she said.

Penny sat by her. "Are you thinking of becoming a volunteer?" she asked.

"Well, not exactly, but it gave me an idea. You see, I was in the shop this morning, and I met Fred Jackson."

"Him as used to work on the railway?"

"Yes, that's the one. Well, he's missing the outdoor life he used to lead, and I've been trying to think of something to help him."

"Volunteering in the shop you mean?" Penny asked, putting her cup back on the tray.

"I don't think working in the shop would suit him, but I wondered if he could do some volunteer gardening if anyone needed it."

"That's a good idea," Penny said, "we've got quite a lot of old people in the village, they might like some help."

The next morning, Annalicia went to the shop to get her newspaper and the groceries she needed as usual.

This morning, Tom Collier was in the shop, buying some yoghurt as she walked in.

"Morning Tom," she said as the girl behind the counter handed her the newspaper without her asking.

"You don't look very happy," she looked at his dismal face.

Tom put the yoghurt down on the counter. "What is there to be happy about?"

"That doesn't sound like you, Tom. What's the matter?"

Annalicia suddenly had a sense that all this had happened before, but this was a different man.

Tom rubbed his ample tummy, "I'm on a diet. My missus made me come out and buy this stuff."

He indicated the pot of natural yoghurt on the counter.

"I'm on a starvation diet," he said, "What I really want is a good meal of roast beef and Yorkshire, but she won't cook it for me. I have to make do with lettuce and yoghurt."

Annalicia looked suitably concerned and made an instant decision.

"Come over to my place at lunchtime, Tom. I'll make you a good meal."

"That's kind of you, Anna, but if the missus found out, there would be hell to play."

"You come, Tom. Half past twelve, my place."

Tom's face lit up, "Thanks Anna, I'll be there." He put the yoghurt back on the shelf and marched out, head held high.

Oh dear, Annalicia thought, now what have I done! She suddenly remembered that you should never interfere between a husband and wife. She mentally shrugged and set about choosing things to give him a good meal. Fortunately, the shop was well stocked, so she bought two chops from the freezer and a good fresh broccoli; she had potatoes from her own garden. She hesitated for a moment, then chose a pot of vanilla ice cream.

That will go well with the apple pie I baked yesterday, she thought.

The assistant loaded them into a bag, she paid for them and made her way back to Diggers Bottom.

Come twelve-thirty and she had the meal ready.

There was a knock at the door, and as she opened it, Tom slid in, looking furtive.

"I told the missus I was going over to the allotment," he said.

"Sit yourself down," Annalicia pointed to a kitchen chair.

"Thanks, Anna," he said and was soon tucking into the meal she had prepared. At the end, he sat back rubbing his tummy. "That was good," he said.

"Come again any time," Annalicia took his empty plate.

"I must go," he said. "I'm working on my allotment this afternoon."

He got up and shook Annalicia's hand.

"Anytime I can do you a good turn, let me know."

Annalicia waved him off down the path and went back to clear up. She hadn't eaten with him as she ate very little at lunchtime, her main meal being in the evening.

After washing up, she put on her gardening gloves and went out to do a bit of weeding.

Time went on as she gathered up the weeds and put them in her compost bin.

To her surprise, at about five o'clock, her garden gate clicked open, and Mrs Collier came up the path, looking cross.

"What have you done to my Tom?" she yelled, waving her walking stick.

"Calm down, Mrs Collier," Annalicia said. "What's wrong?"

She put down her hoe and pulled off her gardening gloves.

"You'd best come in for a minute. What's wrong?"

"What's wrong indeed," Ira Collier said. "Only that you've landed my husband in hospital."

Annalicia leaned against the garden wall, "What happened?" she asked.

"You may well ask," Ira said. "After that meal you gave him at lunchtime, he went off to work in his allotment where he collapsed with stomach pains, and they had to rush him to the hospital."

Annalicia invited her in and sat her down. "It can't have been the meal," she said, "unless it was something to do with the chops I bought from the shop."

"All I know is he confessed to me that he'd had a meal at your place, then after I'd given him a telling off, he went to work on his allotment. The first I heard was young Jimmy Sparrow rushing in and saying Tom's taken bad, could I come. When I got there, he was doubled up, clutching his stomach. We got the ambulance, and they whisked him off to the hospital. I came to give you a piece of my mind, but on the way, I calmed down. You were only trying to help, but it must have been the chops you fed him."

"I obviously made the wrong decision, but let's wait and see, shall we? How about a nice cup of tea?" said Annalicia.

As she was going into the kitchen, the phone rang. Annalicia picked it up.

"It's for you, it's the hospital," she said.

Ira took the phone, "I left word I might be down here and gave them your number. I hope you don't mind."

Annalicia waved a hand, "No problem," she said.

"Hallo, what?" Mrs Collier grasped the phone tightly, "Will he be alright?"

As she put the phone down, she was shaking. Annalicia led her to a chair.

"Sit yourself down, and I'll make that cup of tea now."

Tea made, Ira got a grip on herself.

"It turns out it wasn't your fault," she said, "It could have happened any time, but it was lucky it happened when it did. He has to have surgery, but he's going to be alright."

She held her head in her hands and cried.

Annalicia patted her gently on the back.

Annalicia went to see Tom in the hospital, where he was sitting up, chirpy as anything.

"Hello Anna," he said, "that was a good meal you gave me, wasn't it!"

Annalicia grinned, "Well, it got you off the diet."

"Don't make me laugh," he said, holding his stomach.

"Sorry, Tom," she said. "You'll be out of here soon. Do you have to take it easy?"

"That's the idea," he said, "I don't think I'll be working on the allotment for quite a while. I don't know what to do about it really."

Annalicia thought for a minute and then made a decision.

"Fred Jackson wants something to keep him occupied. I could suggest he keeps it going for you?"

Tom looked startled. "I couldn't pay him," he said in alarm.

"I don't think that will be necessary," she said. "Leave it with me. I'll have a word."

Fred was happy to help with the allotment, and when they heard about it, six other people in the village also wanted to help.

"It's good for people to till the soil," Annalicia told her neighbour Penny. "It's a large allotment, so everyone will be happy to share the produce. Tom doesn't have to do anything until he's better and he will get his share."

That evening, Annalicia sat in her rocking chair.

All's well that ends well. I did make the right decision, and there's a new sense of togetherness in the village, she thought.

Vegetable Marrows

Fred laboured up the hill, clutching his vegetable marrow carefully tucked under one arm. He was heading towards the field behind St Stephens church where they were holding the annual fete and flower show. Actually, it was a flower and vegetable show, but they always called it the flower show. The sun shone down in a cloudless August sky, the perfect day for the fete. A thrush was warbling its heart out. All felt good with the world.

"Either this hill is getting higher, or I'm getting older," Fred said aloud to no one in particular as he trudged onwards.

He was startled when a voice replied, "It's time you took it easy, young Fred."

He looked back, and there, following him, was the village's oldest inhabitant, Foxy Sparrow.

No one knew exactly how old Foxy was or, indeed, what his first name really was, but he was generally acknowledged to be the oldest inhabitant in Barrow Magna.

"Hello, Foxy," Fred slowed down to let Foxy catch up with him.

"Off to put your marrow in the show, are you?" Foxy panted.

A more unlike pair you have never seen. Fred, a tall, lanky seventy-year-old, still with a full head of hair, Foxy, a short, shambly sort of person, with just a few wisps of white hair clinging to his scalp.

They walked on silently until they reached the Lych-gate of the church when Fred politely opened it for Foxy to go first.

They went through the churchyard, past the old gravestones and into the field beyond. People from the village were already setting up their stalls.

Fred said goodbye to Foxy who was off to help his sister on a Bring and Buy stall. He walked on into the big tent. The smell of canvas, mown grass and scents from the flowers wafted in the air as he walked through to the back, where the vegetables were being laid out.

"Exhibiting again?" Ralph Jackson, a short, fat, jolly person, landlord of the local pub, 'The Crown' and organiser of the vegetable section, waved his clipboard. "Old Tom has put his marrow in again, but he doesn't stand a chance against Martha Pearse." He looked carefully at Fred's marrow. It was a good shape with creamy-coloured streaks running along its length. A proper marrow.

"Yours looks a good one," he said. "Put it over there by Martha's."

Fred looked at where Ralph had indicated, and there, next to the space where he was to put his marrow, was the largest, most beautiful marrow Fred had ever seen. It was large, pure green and glistened in the light of the tent.

"I don't think my marrow stands a chance against that one, Ralph," he said looking at it with awe, "Martha Pearse always beats me."

"What is it, three years now?" Ralph smiled. "Martha certainly has a knack for growing them."

"Well," grumbled Fred, "She ain't got anything else to do, has she since her Jack died."

"Don't you believe it," Ralph looked up at him in surprise. "She's the life and soul of the Women's Institute. If you go over to their stall, you'll see her marrow and ginger jam. I've tried some, it's delicious." He rubbed his tummy.

"I might do that," Fred said, "but she's going to beat me again with that there marrow." He looked at it with envy.

"See you later," He turned and walked towards the exit, past the carrots, turnips and potatoes, past the mass of flowers and at the end of the tent, past a display of bonsai, where, to his surprise, he saw Foxy.

"I didn't know you were interested in this sort of thing," he said, tapping his friend on the shoulder.

Foxy straightened up, "I just nipped in to have a look at them. Martha Pearse was talking about them at the Women's Institute meeting last week."

Fred laughed, "I didn't know you went to the Women's Institute, Foxy."

"There's a lot you don't know about me," Foxy winked. "No, Martha was telling me about them when I dropped into her place with some manure the other day."

Fred was immediately interested, "What sort of manure would that be?" he asked.

"You still trying to get the secrets of her marrow?"

"Yes, she's going to beat me again this year. Have you seen her marrow? It's a beauty."

Foxy looked cunning. "I don't think it's the manure you should worry about. It's from my sister's riding stable. Just plain ordinary manure. She must have another secret. You'll have to ask her."

"I can't do that. It's probably a professional secret."

"Well, if I were you, I'd just ask. She can only refuse to tell you." Foxy put down the small bonsai tree he had been examining, waved goodbye and walked out of the tent.

Fred pottered about looking at the other exhibits for a while, thinking about what Foxy had said.

Maybe he's right, he thought. *It's driving me crazy. I've got to find out one way or another.*

He walked out of the tent and over to where Foxy was helping Rose lay out things in her stall. Rose was Foxy's younger sister, a fresh-faced, square-set, sensible woman wearing a tweed jacket, looking as if she had just come off a horse.

She greeted him as he came up to the stall, "Fred, how's the marrow?"

"Don't talk to me about marrows," he said, picking up an ornamental brass bowl. "Martha's going to beat me again this year."

"You should ask her what her secret is," Rose came around the side of the stall.

"That's just what Foxy was saying," Fred put the bowl down and looked down the row of stalls. "I think I might go and have a look at the Women's Institute stall.

Foxy chuckled. "Like as not you're going to buy some of Martha's marrow jam. I see she's down at the stall."

"Maybe so," Fred said. He turned and walked down, past a stall selling hot dogs, a raffle stall, a stall selling pictures painted by the artist herself until, finally, he reached the Women's Institute stall, where a cluster of women were fussing over the arrangement of the items. Head and shoulders above the others, Martha Pearse, dressed in a workmanlike apron, was busy, arranging jars of jam.

As Fred came up, she came round the stall to greet him. "Hello, Fred, did you bring a marrow this year?"

Fred looked grumpily at her, "Yes, I did, and so did old Tom, but you're going to beat both of us again. I've never seen such a beauty as the one you've put in."

"Cheer up," she said. "You never know what will happen. Have you heard? We've got a new judge this year. A Mrs Pettit, just moved here from up North. Supposed to be real hot stuff at judging."

"I did hear, but I ain't seen her yet." He looked down at the array of jam jars. "Foxy was telling me you make some of your marrows into jam."

Martha smiled, "Marrow and ginger. Do you want to try a jar?"

"I'd like to if it's not too expensive."

"Here," she said, "Have one on me." She handed him a jar.

"I can't take that," Fred protested, "Let me pay you for it."

"Go on, take it," Martha insisted.

"Well, thank you kindly," he said, "You must let me know if I can do anything for you."

"Let's wait until after the judging," she said. "Now you'll have to excuse me. I've got to get the stall sorted out."

She turned away, and Fred wandered off down to the tea tent, where he had a cup of tea and a piece of chocolate cake, gazing out at the busy scene. People were coming in now, and some of the stalls were doing a good trade. He could see Foxy and Rose busy on their Bring and Buy stall. Looking at his watch, he knew that the judging would take place in about ten minutes' time. He didn't want to rush over to see what had happened, so he timed himself so that he would arrive in the Flower and Vegetable tent just after the judging.

He looked at his watch again, and it was time.

When he reached the tent, walking through to the vegetable section, he could see that, for some reason, the judges were still deliberating. The two usual judges, Ralph and the other judge, Mr Blackett, were arguing with a colourfully dressed lady in a vivid purple hat, obviously Mrs Pettit.

"I can't believe what you're saying," Ralph held a gold medal card in his hand. "We always award Martha Pearse the best marrow. Just look at it, it beats the others by a long way."

"I know it looks good," Helen Pettit said. "But it's not a marrow, it's a courgette."

At that point Martha came into the tent and, striding across to where the judges were standing, said in a loud voice, "So, you've guessed my secret. Of course, it's a courgette, but if you look this up, you'll see that if you leave a courgette long enough, you get a marrow. What's wrong with that?"

Mr Blackett coughed, "Well, if it is a courgette, then we can't award it first prize. So, the gold medal must go to Fred Mimms this year for the best marrow."

Martha clapped him on the back. "There you are Fred, first prize at last."

"Martha," he said, "You don't seem to mind. If it were me, I'd be flaming mad."

"Well, Fred, the way I see it, I've won the prize for three years. It was about time someone else had it, and I'd rather it went to you than anyone else." She looked pointedly at old Tom who had come up behind them.

"You two," Tom said. "It's alright for you, but my marrow always gets third place. It's not fair." He stumped off.

"There's one jealous old man," Martha said, taking Fred's hand and shaking it. "You won fair and square. Don't worry about him."

Fred looked at her in a new light. *I'd always thought she was one of those bossy women who had to have their own way, but maybe I was wrong*, he thought.

"Thanks, Martha," he said. He now saw her as a woman he could call a friend. Maybe more than that.

He walked out of the tent, his heart singing with his victory.

But in 'The Crown' that night, old Tom was holding forth.

"It ain't fair," he said as he took hold of his pint, talking to anyone who would listen.

Foxy was sitting in his usual spot by the fire, and his ears pricked up when he heard Fred's name mentioned.

"I reckon," Tom said, wiping the froth off his mouth. "I reckon Martha Pearse is sweet on Fred Mimms."

"How so?" asked Ralph Jackson, the publican, leaning over the bar.

"Well, you were at the fete this afternoon." Tom lifted his glass.

"As you know, I put my marrow in as usual, and so did Martha and Fred. Martha always wins, but this year, she let Fred win. You mark my words, there's something going on between them."

Foxy turned towards the bar. "Don't you take no heed of old Tom. He's just jealous 'cos he didn't win."

Foxy was right, but unfortunately, once a rumour starts in a village like Barrow Magna, it spreads like wildfire.

"Martha's sweet on Fred Mimms."

"I always knew something was going on between them."

"It just shows you. Her husband's only been dead a year, and here she is going on something terrible with Fred Mimms."

As the rumour travelled around the village, it got worse and worse until it came to the ears of Martha herself.

"Load of nonsense," she said in the next meeting of the Women's Institute. "Just because Fred won the best marrow and that Mrs Pettit discovered my secret doesn't mean anything. But I know what I have to do from now on." And she did.

Next time she met Fred in the high street, she passed him by without a glance.

It was a lovely August morning, the birds were in full song, and Fred was in his front garden.

"Wonder what's wrong with Martha?" Fred, busy weeding his flower bed, leaned on his spade as Foxy stopped for a chat. "I thought she was a friend of mine, but it don't seem like it."

Foxy grinned, "You ain't heard the rumours, then?"

"No, what?"

"Folks are saying that she deliberately let you win the best marrow and that she's sweet on you."

"So, that's why she's avoiding me." Fred stamped his spade into the soil. "We can't have that. Thanks, Foxy, I'm going to do something about this."

When Fred had finished, he cleaned his spade and put it back in the shed. He thought long and hard about what he should do. His first thought was just to let her go on ignoring him, but then he decided he ought to go and have it out with her.

But what excuse can I have to go and see her? he thought.

Not a man to rush into anything, he made himself a cup of coffee and sat down at his kitchen table to think. His eye lighted on the jar of jam that Martha had given him at the fete. He had been enjoying its subtle mix of marrow and ginger as a breakfast treat. The jar was only half-empty but an idea began to form in his mind.

How about if I go to see her and ask if she can sell me another jar?

His mind made up, he put on a clean shirt and his best jacket and walked over to Diggers Bottom where Martha had her cottage.

He made his way up the paved path to the front door. A bed full of sweet-smelling flowers waved in the breeze as he passed by as though to say, *Hello Fred, welcome.*

A blackbird crossed the front lawn, looking for worms.

He gave the ornamental knocker a gentle tap and then when nothing happened, a harder one. There was a pause, and the door opened. Martha was standing there, rubbing her hands on a towel.

As soon as she saw who it was, a frown crossed her usually sunny face, and she started to close the door.

Fred, remembering the usual salesman's trick, stuck his foot in the door.

"Wait, Martha, I need to talk to you."

She opened the door a little wider, "What's there to talk about?"

Fred decided to be honest, "I was going to pretend I'd come to ask for another jar of your gorgeous jam, but what I've really come about is to say I'm sorry that people are spreading rumours about us and came to see if I could make amends in some way."

Martha's gaze softened, "You'd better come in then. I was just going to make a cup of tea. Would you like one? I've got freshly baked scones just out of the oven."

"Sounds a treat," Fred walked into Martha's neat and tidy front room.

"Come on through to the kitchen. We can talk there."

Fred suddenly became nervous. It had seemed the right thing to do, but now that he was actually sitting down in Martha's kitchen with the real person in front of him, he found himself tongue-tied.

Martha bustled around, setting a scone and a cup of tea in front of him.

"Now, what's this all about?" she asked, settling herself in her rocking chair in front of the stove.

"You know as well as I do," he said, biting into his scone. "It's about the rumours that someone is spreading about you and me."

"Yes, I've heard," Martha wriggled in her chair. "I shouldn't have ignored you the other day, but I was so uptight about the rumour that's going around. You and I know it's not true."

"What exactly have you heard?" Fred put his cup down.

"That I deliberately lost the marrow competition because…" she hesitated.

"Because you were interested in me," Fred finished for her.

"Well, yes, but I'm not, am I," Martha blushed.

"I don't know about that," Fred felt his own temperature rising, "but has it ever occurred to you," and he took his courage in both hands, "has it ever occurred to you that I might be interested in you?"

Martha's blush widened. "I don't know what you mean, Fred." She sat forward in her seat.

"I mean since the village thinks we're, you know, why not really give them something to gossip about," Fred went over to her and held her hand.

"You're a very attractive woman, Martha, and we're both on our own. Why not give it a try?"

Martha squeezed his hand, "I'll give it some thought. In the meantime, have another jar of my jam to take home and keep you company."

A Fish Out of Water

"Hot chocolate and a piece of lemon drizzle cake, please." Susan had come over from Barrow Magna to the book café in Cirencester as she always did on a Thursday. She took her tray to a small table near the window, put her handbag by her feet and settled down to enjoy her weekly treat.

The book café was a hub of activity. A young mother, bouncing her baby up and down, people texting on their mobile phones, some looking earnestly at computer screens, others reading books.

Susan was reading a book about quests, where the hero, if he survived, would bring back the treasure to the king so that he could marry his daughter type of thing.

She sipped her hot chocolate. I wish someone would go on a quest for me, she thought.

Suddenly a figure loomed over her, stumbled, and a book dropped in her lap. Startled, she read the title, "Fly Fishing".

A good-looking young man peered anxiously at her.

"Sorry about that," he said. "I tripped over your handbag."

He was balancing a cup of coffee in one hand and trying to take the book with the other.

"Sit down," she said, handing him the book, waving at the seat opposite, "you'll spill your coffee."

"Sorry about the book. I was going to have a read and a coffee."

Susan suppressed a smile as he sat down, "That's okay," she said. "Are you a clever fisherman?"

He looked puzzled.

"You don't know?' she said. "Fly means knowing or clever. Are you clever at fishing?"

"I see," he laughed. "No, not yet, but I mean to learn, and in any case, fly fishing means using artificial flies as bait."

"Oh!" she said, "Not my subject, but I'm reading this." She held up her book to cover her confusion.

"Looks interesting, but I'm interrupting you," he said, looking at her over the book. "Do go on reading."

Susan suddenly felt warm inside. It's the hot chocolate, she thought. "I'm Susan Long."

"Neil Farmer."

They shook hands.

I wonder if he's married, Susan thought. She saw him trying to look at her left hand and guessed that he wasn't.

They read for a while, then, when she had eaten the last of her cake and finished her drink, she got up.

"I must go. Nice to meet you. Good luck with your fishing."

He looked up, putting his book on the table. "I say, I mean, could we meet or see each other again?"

That's a bit forward, Susan thought, but he is handsome and friendly.

"Why not invite me when you do some fly fishing? I live in Barrow Magna," she said, smiling.

He looked at her seriously. "I must read the book and get the gear, but yes, why not? Can I phone to fix a date?"

They exchanged phone numbers.

He watched her leave the shop. She looked back and waved.

A week went by, but no phone calls.

Susan began to think it was just a chance encounter, and then on Saturday morning, she got a call.

"Neil Farmer. We have a date to go fishing."

"Yes, we do," she said breathlessly.

"I've read the book and got the gear. Will you come on Sunday?"

"Fine, I'll make a picnic," she said.

"Give me your address, I'll pick you up," he said. "How about eight o'clock in the morning?"

"You're joking. How about ten thirty."

She gave him her address, "Number Ten, Diggers Bottom, Barrow Magna."

The doorbell rang at exactly ten thirty, Sunday morning.

He was dressed like a fisherman, floppy hat and long mac, but ordinary shoes.

He saw her looking down. "I've left my waders and tackle in the car," he explained.

His car was an old, open tourer. He carried her picnic basket to the car.

"I thought we would go to a river that I know," he said, putting the basket in the back.

"Fine by me," Susan got in, settling back to enjoy the ride.

It was a lovely day, small white clouds edged lazily across the sky. Neil turned the car down a narrow track, parking it by a number of other cars in an area close to the river.

The river widened into shallows at that point, and Susan could see other figures standing in the water a short distance away.

"I've brought a ground sheet," he said. "I thought it might be a bit damp, sitting on the grass."

"I didn't realise you would be standing in the river. I thought you just did it from the bank?"

"No, fly fishing is different. You wade out and cast your line into the water."

Susan looked at the other figures. "The other anglers look like men on their own. Don't their wives or girlfriends ever come with them to fish?"

Neil laughed, "No woman in their right mind would want to wait for hours hoping to land a fish."

Susan smiled. "It's going to be boring, is it?"

"No, I didn't mean that," he said his face colouring up. "You did suggest coming."

"Right," she said. "Let's see the expert at work."

She could tell he was nervous as he put on his waders and prepared his rod.

He took out a tin containing some feathery things and put one of them on his fishing line.

"What are those?" Susan asked.

"They're artificial flies. You put one on the line, make a cast and keep moving the fly about on the surface like a real fly until you get a bite."

He waded out into the centre of the shallow water, waved at her and cast his line.

Susan wanted to help him as he looked so nervous, but after a few goes, she could tell he was getting more confident.

Time passed, but no fish seemed to want to be caught.

After watching for a while, Susan called to him and suggested that they might have lunch. She opened her basket and spread out the things she had brought, ham sandwiches, roast chicken-flavoured crisps, a bottle of chardonnay, with peaches for afters. Napkins, plates, and glasses for the white wine.

Neil waded out of the water and propped his rod against a convenient tree trunk.

"Thank you for preparing such a sumptuous picnic," he said, munching happily. "I think I'll call it a day. It wasn't very exciting, was it? I obviously haven't got the hang of it yet. I ought to take you back," he said with concern.

After they had eaten, Susan began packing up the picnic.

Neil packed his rod and tackle and rolled up the ground sheet.

As they stood up, he looked at her quizzically. "I know this wasn't a success, but may I ask you out again, perhaps for dinner?"

Susan felt her eyes sparkle. She said, "I'd love to, but remember the book I was reading about quests?"

"What's that got to do with going out?" He looked puzzled.

"I'm sending you on a quest before I agree to go out with you again."

Neil looked alarmed.

"Don't worry, all you have to do is bring me a fish that you caught yourself by Saturday."

Neil looked thoughtful, then he turned to her and smiled, "Okay, I'll do it."

Late on Saturday, the doorbell rang. It was Neil, and in his hands lay a large fish wrapped in paper.

"Will you come out with me tonight?" he asked.

"Yes, I promised. Now tell me about your catch."

"No," he said, "Wait until tonight. I know a good fish restaurant, 'The Fisherman's Plaice'. I'll come for you at seven if that's alright."

Susan smiled to herself, "Yes, I know the restaurant, it's good. I'll be ready."

Neil gave the fish to the Maitre'd as they went in. "Give this to the chef. I phoned earlier," he said.

As the waiter settled them at a corner table, a white-coated figure wearing a chef's hat came over. Neil stood and shook hands. He introduced Susan.

"This is my friend Susan. She's the one who challenged me to produce the fish."

"Ah, mademoiselle, the fish, it is magnificent, but not as magnificent as that fish," he looked at a large pike mounted above the bar, winking at Susan. "But surely the best I have seen."

Later the chef himself brought the plates to the table. "I have given you 'trout a la almonde," he said.

The filleted fish lay in a bed of almonds with lemon wedges. Jersey Royal potatoes, broccoli and carrots sat close in serving dishes.

"Wonderful," said Susan as the lemony aroma rose. She thanked the chef, then she turned to Neil and asked, "Did you really catch this fish yourself?"

Neil wriggled uncomfortably. "Well, you see, my father runs a trout farm."

"So, you cheated?"

"No, not exactly. I caught it with my bare hands from one of my father's tanks."

Susan turned her head away, and then, unable to contain herself, she burst out laughing. "You are a clever fisherman," she said, "but so am I." She pointed to the large pike. "I caught that when I was twelve. Of course, my father helped me land it. He owns this restaurant. So, you see, we are both clever fishermen."

A Song of Love

Suzy, a bouncy twelve-year-old girl with golden hair, had come back from singing in the Barrow Magna school choir. She kissed her Mum, Elaine, dumped her satchel on a chair, sat down on a kitchen chair and announced, "I want to be a singer when I grow up."

Elaine stopped rolling out the pastry she was making for a pie, looked up and said, "Whatever makes you want to do that?"

Suzy got up and skipped around the kitchen, stopping to look up at Elaine with wide innocent eyes.

"My teacher says I have a good voice and ought to make something of it. You were a singer before you married Daddy, weren't you?"

Elaine put down her rolling pin, wiped her hands on her apron and, for a moment, wondered what to say. Then she decided. "Yes I was, but it was a hard life and not one I would recommend anyone to follow."

Elaine had been a cabaret artist before she married. She remembered the bad times when trying to get singing engagements. Meeting her husband, Bob, falling in love and having Suzy, their only child, had seemed like a miracle. She had gone on singing for a while but then felt that she must give up her career to look after her family. She had vowed that her daughter would never have to struggle as she had done.

Discussing it with Bob that night, she said, "She can be anything she likes, but don't let her be a singer. I know how hard it can be."

Bob looked admiringly at Elaine, "But you have a wonderful voice," he said. "I've often wondered why you gave it up after you met me."

"I didn't want to, but when Suzy came along, I decided to devote all my energies to both of you." She pressed his hand and looked into his eyes. "I love you and our daughter very much, but singing isn't for her."

"I love you too, but as Suzy grows up, you must let her make her own way in life," he said.

"I know, but I want to shield her from what I went through."

Next day, Elaine decided that the only way she could handle the situation was to be honest and warn Suzy of the dangers.

When she spoke to Suzy, she said, "I know what your teacher said, but she probably has never had the bad experiences I had. It costs a lot of money to train, and it is a very precarious life. Not one I would want a daughter of mine to follow."

Suzy cried that night, but fortunately, she had two friends who were more supportive.

At weekends, Suzy helped Pauline and Effie in the Muddy Moles Teashop.

One of their weekend customers was Alfredo, a balding Italian tenor, and his English wife, Amanda. As they sat drinking their coffee, Alfredo would quietly sing arias from great Italian operas. The other customers loved it, and it got Suzy into the habit of singing as she served. From Alfredo, she began to learn the great songs.

When she told him what her mother had said, he looked down at the twelve-year-old girl, patted her golden hair and looked at her clear blue eyes so full of hope.

"You can be anything you want to be, my love. We hear you singing in the café. Amanda and I love your singing."

Suzy looked up at him and smiled, "But Mum says I can never be a singer. Why does she say that?"

Alfredo looked thoughtful. "I was told that your Mum was a singer years ago, but I think she had a hard time. She doesn't want you to go the same way."

Suzy's other friend, Paul, was just a little bit older than her. They had grown up together and shared all their secrets.

"I don't see why you couldn't be a singer if you want to," he said, sounding very grownup. "I want to be a successful businessman when I'm older, and I shall come and sweep you off your feet."

Suzy laughed, "Perhaps I'll sweep you off your feet."

Suzy didn't mention her idea again at home, but the more she talked to Alfredo and Paul, the more determined she became.

One weekend, Alfredo came up to her and said, "I don't know if you've noticed, but there's a show on at the theatre in Cirencester tomorrow, and they've announced a singing competition. Anyone local can enter. Why don't you try. There's a prize and you could well win."

"I couldn't do it without telling Mum," Suzy said.

She told her that afternoon, and, to her surprise, Elaine didn't reject the idea out of hand. "I'll have to ask your father," she said.

Elaine really wanted Bob to agree with her that Suzy shouldn't take part, but when she told him, Bob said, "You should let her try. It won't do any harm."

Elaine argued at first but then gave in and, once committed, gave Suzy every help she could.

At first, Suzy wanted to sing one of the songs Alfredo had taught her, but Elaine, knowing that a small girl should sing something popular and appropriate for a local audience, persuaded her to sing 'Over the Rainbow'. Elaine helped her rehearse it.

Meanwhile, Alfredo entered her name in the competition, and she was to sing second out of four competitors.

When she told Paul, he was delighted. "You'll be a famous singer one day, and I'll come to hear you."

Suzy was very nervous. She spent the day rehearsing and rehearsing until Elaine had to tell her to stop. "You'll strain your voice. Just rest for a while."

Suzy could not rest, she felt so excited, but then it was time to get dressed and go to the show.

Elaine let her dress in her party frock, a simple blue dress with a wide white collar, rather like a picture of Alice from Alice in Wonderland.

Suzy huddled into her warm coat as her parents took her to the theatre. It was a stormy night, and Suzy was glad to get inside where it was warm and comfortable. They went round the side where a young woman holding a clipboard greeted them.

"Yes, competitor number two. Come with me."

She led Suzy through a door at the back into the space behind the stage, sitting her down on a low bench.

"Hello young woman, what's your name?" A large red-faced man bent over her.

"I'm Suzy, and I've come to sing," she said.

"I'm Martin," he said with a smile. "Hi, Suzy. I look after the show, and I will be introducing you. Sit tight for now."

It was quite interesting at first, as Suzy was able to see everyone getting ready. Three other people lined up with her on the bench, looking nervous. One was a man who looked old to Suzy but probably wasn't, there was another girl about Suzy's age and a tall, thin woman dressed in what looked like a tent.

The show began, and sounds of it echoed through to the back of the stage. Then it was time for the competition. The tall, thin woman was on first, and she sang an aria from Madam Butterfly. Her voice was shrill and high-pitched. There was some applause, and she came off quickly, red in the face.

The young woman with the clipboard came and led Suzy into the wings. "You're on," she said, giving her a push.

Martin was already on stage. Putting his arm around her shoulder, he said, "Please welcome Suzy, who will sing 'Over the Rainbow' from the Wizard of Oz."

There was real hearty applause as Martin moved her gently up to the microphone. She stood there petrified, looking out at the sea of faces. By the light of the footlights, she could just see her parents, with Alfredo and Paul in the front row.

Martin gave her a hug. "Right Suzy, go."

The pianist struck a note, there was a hush, and Suzy opened her mouth to sing. To her horror, only a small, strangled noise came out. What could be wrong? Her voice that afternoon had been perfect. The thought went through her mind, perhaps her mother was right, she couldn't be a singer. She began to panic.

She could see Paul in the audience looking worried. The more she tried, the worse it was. The audience started to become restive. A slow handclap started. Suzy turned to look at Martin who shrugged his shoulders at her as though to say, "What's the matter?" She looked at the audience and rushed off the stage in tears.

The rest of the evening was a blur to her. Later, she found out that the older man had won the competition. He had sung 'Asleep in the Deep', but Suzy got no sleep that night. She lay in bed, crying her eyes out.

Elaine was sympathetic but was quietly glad that things had turned out the way they had.

"I know what it's like standing out there in front of all those people. I felt so sorry for her, but that should change her mind about being a singer," she said to Bob after putting Suzy to bed, but she didn't know Suzy.

Suzy stood looking out into the darkness of the theatre. The front row of people were just visible beyond the orchestra pit.

The conductor rapped his baton and the music began.

Suzy gripped the microphone and began to sing.

The song was an old one, wafting melodies of long ago across the audience. As she sang, it was as though the theatre had disappeared and she stood alone in the midst of a forest, mist outlining the trees, a river at her feet. Leisurely, leisurely the song drifted on. As she sang, her mind went back to when, as a little girl, she had wanted to be a singer and how her first appearance on stage had been so disastrous.

That was a long time ago, but she remembered how Alfredo had convinced her mother that she should go to the local School of Music and had offered to pay her fees. Suzy's mother, Elaine, refused at first until he suggested that it was only a loan and that Suzy could pay him back when successful.

Suzy's career had been a success. She had sung at the London Opera House and the Glasgow Royal Concert Hall and had taken leading roles in opera houses across Europe.

Tonight was a very special night for her. She was back in Cirencester at the theatre giving a special concert for charity.

As she sang, she looked at the front row of the stalls. There, in the front, were her parents, Elaine and Bob, an older-looking Alfredo with his wife Amanda, and next to them was Paul.

The song ended, the audience was enthusiastic. The applause rolled over her. She bowed and made to leave the stage. The audience wouldn't let her go, they demanded an encore.

She turned, walked back to the microphone, nodding to the conductor. As she looked out at her parents and Paul, she began to sing, "Somewhere over the rainbow bluebirds sing …" The song ended. She took a bow. The audience rose to their feet clapping. Paul, her husband, clapped looking at her with love and admiration.

The little girl who had fled from that stage all those years ago was no more.

Letters From a Son

Emily Pitcher lived alone in the Cotswold village of Barrow Magna. Every week, on a Friday morning, the postman called with a letter. It was from her son in London.

Emily worked as a volunteer in the village shop and used to share the contents of her letters with her coworker, Florence. They were full of news about what was happening and how her son was getting on. Florence loved to listen when Emily shared the letters with her.

There came a day when Emily didn't appear in the shop. After work, Florence went to Emily's house, a thatched cottage in Diggers Bottom. She knocked at the door. There was no answer, but the door swung open. Hunched over the table where she had been writing, was Emily.

Florence went up to her and tapped on her shoulder. "Wake up Emily," she said, thinking she had fallen asleep, but Emily had passed away.

The news of her passing spread through the village. Many were heartbroken to learn that the woman, whom they had come to know as such a gentle soul, had lived a life of loneliness with only her son's letters to comfort her.

Florence realised they must let the son know of Emily's death. So, as she helped clear the house and pack up Emily's belongings, she came across a box of letters—the ones she had received from her son each week.

She opened one of the letters to find the son's address.

Florence took it upon herself to write to the son at the address on the letter to let him know that the funeral would be in two weeks, could he come?

The letter came back a few days later, "Not known at this address."

Looking again at the letters, Florence noticed that they were written in Emily's handwriting. She then realised that Emily must have written the letters to herself. There was no son.

What she had done was create a world of her own, filled with the love and care she had always longed for.

Florence decided to share the secret of the letters with the rest of the village. They were amazed at Emily's creativity and her ability to find happiness in solitude.

After the funeral, which the whole village attended, the village booked a time each week in the village hall where people could come to share their own stories of loneliness and isolation, and it became a place where people could find comfort and companionship.

As more and more people joined the group, the village came alive with a newfound sense of community and togetherness. The woman who had once lived a life of solitude had unknowingly sparked a revolution of love and inclusivity within the village.

It was a chilly winter's evening when the village shop's doorbell rang. Florence was about to close the shop and rush home to her warm house, but the sight of a dishevelled young man standing at the door made her hesitate.

"Can I help you?" she asked, her eyes scanning the man's worn-out shoes and ragged coat.

"I'm looking for Mrs Pitcher," the man said, his voice trembling.

Florence's heart sank. "I'm sorry, sir," she said, trying to keep her voice steady. "Mrs Pitcher passed away."

The man's face fell. "Oh no," he murmured. "Then I am too late."

Florence frowned. "Do you know Mrs Pitcher?" she asked, her curiosity piqued.

The man nodded slowly. "She was my mother," he said, his eyes brimming with tears. "I've been searching for her for years. I saw the obituary notice in your local paper and wondered if it was my mother and, now, I can never say goodbye."

Florence's heart went out to the man. She knew how it felt to lose someone and never get the chance to say goodbye.

The man took a deep breath and wiped his eyes. "My mother and I had a falling out a long time ago," he said. "I was young and foolish, and I said things I didn't mean. I wanted to make amends and tell her that I love her, but I didn't know where she was."

Florence nodded understandingly. "I'm sorry you didn't get the chance to see her again," she said. "But if it's any consolation, your mother was a wonderful woman who touched many lives."

The man's eyes widened. "What do you mean?" he asked.

Florence told him about the letters Emily had written to herself and how it had helped the village come together as a community.

"I wish I had found her sooner," he said. "I could have told her how much she meant to me."

Florence put a hand on his shoulder. "I'm sure she knew," she said softly. "Mothers have a way of knowing these things."

Photo Finish

The sun was shining, and the air was full of bird song as Cara walked through Halton Woods outside Barrow Magna. She followed the well-worn track, feeling the soft leaf mould under her feet. Sunlight cast dappled shadows as she made her way through the trees towards the low stone wall separating the woods from the meadow beyond.

She had been in the meadow many times before. It was an enchanted place. Long grass, a myriad of flowers, some poking their heads up through the grass, some so tiny you had to stoop to find them. She reached the wall and climbed over into the meadow. She was so happy she began to sing out loud.

This was her daily exercise walk, a change and a rest from the novel she was writing.

She walked through the long grass, singing at the top of her voice, not looking where she was going, until suddenly she stumbled and fell onto something soft and lumpy. As she picked herself up, the mound stirred and turned itself into a man.

"I'm so sorry," she said, looking down. "Are you alright?"

He groaned as he looked up at her, "What do you think?" he said.

"Let me help you up," she held out her hand.

"No, I think I'll stay here if you don't mind," he searched around for the mobile phone he had dropped.

"Why are you lying on the ground?" she asked. "Are you ill?"

"I might be, now you've trodden on me," he said. "No, I was doing a spot of macro photography. Perhaps I will get up so that I can explain."

He heaved himself to his feet wincing slightly, towering above Cara.

He looked down at her.

"I'm Rudy Van Dorf, and who have I had the pleasure of being stepped on by?"

He held out his hand. Cara shook it.

"I'm Cara, and I'm so sorry, but you must admit it isn't every day you fall over a live body."

Rudy rubbed his chin, "I suppose not, but you see I was photographing this flower." He pointed to a spot on the ground.

Cara looked down. "I can't see anything," she said.

"That's why you need to lie down," he grasped her hand. "Come on."

He pulled her to the ground and lay down beside her.

This is ridiculous, Cara thought, a man I've just met, and here we are lying on the ground together.

The strangeness of the situation didn't seem to bother her companion as he carefully parted the grass between them and raised his mobile phone.

"There she is," he said. "Isn't she a beauty?"

Cara looked carefully at the small red flower set in the grass.

"It is rather gorgeous," she said. "Are you taking a picture of it with that thing?"

She pointed to his strange-looking mobile phone. "I've never seen a phone like that with a bit sticking out."

"It's just an ordinary phone with an extra lens on it. Look, I'll show you."

He pulled at the small circular lens, and it came away, leaving an ordinary mobile phone.

"The lens is a bit loose," he said, fitting it back. "But it takes a terrific close-up picture. Here, I'll show you." He aimed the phone at the flower and clicked. Then, turning it around, showed her the close-up picture of the flower.

"Terrific," she said. "But do you think we ought to move? This ground is damp."

"Thoughtless of me," he said, getting up and offering her a hand. She took it, and he heaved her up. She fell into his arms. "Thank you," she said, pulling away and brushing pollen from her skirt.

She looked carefully at his broad shoulders, his jet-black hair, blue eyes, Roman nose and definitely kissable lips. What a handsome hunk of a man, she thought, giving a little shudder and backing away from him.

They stood there motionless for a moment, as though wondering what to do next, when something slithered through the grass beside them.

Rudy looked down, gave a start, dropped his phone and ran.

"It's a snake! I hate snakes!" he yelled as he ran towards the field gate.

"Wait," Cara picked up his phone and stood still as the snake slithered past.

"Wait, it's only a grass snake, it won't hurt you. You dropped your phone."

It was too late. Rudy had jumped over the gate and was gone.

Cara was still holding the phone, the extra lens had fallen into the long grass. Cara stooped down, trying to find it, but now she knew there were snakes in the grass, she didn't look very carefully. Clutching the phone, she made her way back through the woods to her cottage.

She put the phone down carefully on a side table, still switched on.

When he realises he had left it behind, he is bound to call, she thought.

The rest of the day, she spent working on her novel. The publisher was chasing her to finish it.

As she worked, she kept looking at the phone, but it didn't ring.

Time passed, the novel was finished and dispatched to the publisher.

She kept Rudy's phone in the kitchen drawer, using her own phone's charger to make sure it was charged every few days, hoping that one day he would contact her, but the phone didn't ring.

Then, one day, almost a year later, while preparing the evening meal, she heard a strange ringing sound coming from the kitchen drawer. She opened it, and there was Rudy's phone making a noise. She clicked it on and held it to her ear.

"Is that you?" Rudy asked. "And do you still have my phone?"

"That's a silly question," Cara said. "Would I be answering it if it wasn't your phone? Where have you been all this time?"

"My editor sent me abroad, I'm a war photographer. I meant to contact you but forgot to take the number of my old phone with me. I just got back, found my old phone number, so I rang, hoping you would still have it."

"All year, I've been recharging your phone, but you didn't call," she said accusingly.

"I'm so sorry," he said. "Look, we can't keep talking on the phone. Will you come out with me for a meal?"

Cara paused for a moment, then said, "Yes, I would like that."

"How about tomorrow at seven? I know a good restaurant, 'The Olive Branch'."

Cara laughed "Very appropriate, I know the place. So, see you there tomorrow evening. I'll bring your phone."

Next day, time seemed to drag for Cara, but, eventually, it was time to go. The restaurant was quite upmarket, so she put on her new blue dress and her favourite necklace, a silver chain with a hanging pearl, but she forgot to put his phone in her handbag.

As she arrived at The Olive Branch, she suddenly remembered the phone.

Bother! I can't go back for it. Perhaps it will give me a chance to see him again, she thought.

The table had been booked, and she was shown to it, but Rudy hadn't arrived.

She sat eating the breadsticks. The waiter asked if she wanted a drink while she waited, but she just asked for water.

Time dragged on. At first, it was fun watching the other diners, trying to guess their occupations, and then it wasn't fun anymore. Where was Rudy?

Diners finished their meal and most were leaving; waiters were clearing up and setting the tables for the next day. One came across to Cara.

"Stood you up, has he, love?"

He meant it to be friendly, but Cara, having sat for two hours feeding on breadsticks and water, was in no mood to be friendly.

"Do I owe you anything?" she said crossly, ignoring his comment.

"Of course not. I'm just so sorry he didn't turn up." The waiter was an elderly man who looked at her with compassion.

"So am I," Cara picked up her handbag, smiled at the man and left.

Inside, she was fuming.

Back at home, she took Rudy's phone from the kitchen drawer and dumped it in the wastepaper basket.

"The end of the affair," she said, giving the basket a kick.

As she did so, the phone began to ring. She picked it up. It was Rudy.

"What's the excuse this time?" she shouted into the phone.

"I'm sorry," he said, "My editor sent me off to cover a fire in Newmarket at a racing stable. I tried to phone, but you didn't answer my phone."

"I forgot to take it with me. That's probably why I didn't hear it."

"Well, I took good pictures of the fire," he said lamely.

"Good for you. Now what? I'm throwing this phone away unless you can suggest something sensible."

"No, don't do that," he said. "How about meeting where we met originally?"

"You mean in the meadow where you dragged me to the ground and rushed off with a snake chasing you?"

"Well yes, if you put it like that," he said, with laughter in his voice.

"Well, it is a year later almost to the day, so I suppose we could do the meadow bit as long as you promise not to rush off like last time."

"I promise," he said. "Tomorrow is Saturday. How about midday at the meadow, then if you want to, we could go for a late lunch."

Cara made up her mind quickly, "Fine, see you then."

She put the phone down slowly.

Do I want this? She thought. Why am I bothering with this man?

Then she knew the answer. He's fun and I like the way he deals with things. Except perhaps the snake. I'll go and see what happens.

The sun was shining, and the air was full of birdsong as Cara followed the well-worn path through the woods. She leapt over the low wall into the flower meadow and walked to the spot where she remembered she had met Rudy. There was no sign of him, so she looked down to see if the flower he had shown her had flowered again.

As she did so, something gleaming in the grass caught her eye. She stooped and picked it up.

It was the lens from Rudy's mobile phone. She took his phone out of her handbag and placed the lens on the phone. There was a click, and the lens fitted perfectly.

As she did so, Rudy came towards her, taking the phone from her hand.

They stood motionless for a moment as though wondering what to do next.

"How about lunch?" he said.

Cara looked him up and down. "I know a place," she said. "It's called the Last Chance Pub. Come on, I'm buying. There won't be any snakes in the pub." She reached out and took his hand as something slithered past them in the grass.

How Does Your Garden Grow

Amy parked her bicycle alongside the hedge and stood at the garden gate, almost afraid to go in. She clutched the folder containing her portfolio tightly, clicked the latch and walked up the path, breathing in the scent of newly mown grass. An old man almost bent double with age, straightened up from the flowerbed he was weeding.

"You'll be Miss Carson," he said, shaking hands.

Amy smiled, "Mr Mears, I've heard a lot about you."

"Ah well, I thought it were about time I retired while I've still got some life left in me," he chuckled. "You're a comely lass. How come you want to be a gardener?"

"It's something I've wanted to do all my life," she said. "We didn't have a big garden at home when I was small, so I planted things in pots and put them out in the backyard. Now I'm just about to start my life as a proper gardener."

"Well," he said. "You'd better go up to the house, Mr Jackson's expecting you. Good luck." He went back to his weeding.

Amy walked to the front door of the house.

A rose twined itself carelessly over the front porch, throwing its pale pink blossoms towards her as she rang the doorbell. A muted buzz sounded from somewhere inside.

The door opened, and a tall man appeared, looking down at her.

"Mr Jackson? I'm Amy Carson," she said in a voice that trembled ever so slightly.

"Miss Carson, come in. I was expecting you," he stood aside to let her pass.

"Come into the study, I was just about to have a coffee. Would you like one?"

"Thank you, I would," she said.

He led the way into a comfortable-looking room with shelves covered in books.

As he poured coffee from a flask into two cups, Amy's thoughts were chaotic. *Will he like me? Can I do the job?*

Ralph Jackson picked up his spectacles from the desk and looked at her portfolio.

"You did well at Agricultural College, and you have glowing references from your lecturers. I think you'll do," he said, handing the folder back to her. "When can you start?"

"I can start tomorrow if that's alright," Amy said, a warm glow spreading inside her.

Ralph nodded, "I need a gardener as I write detective stories and don't get time to garden," he put his spectacles on the desk.

Amy smiled, thinking how handsome he looked without his glasses. "I didn't know we had a famous writer in the village," she said.

"You may not have seen any of my books," he looked at the pile of books on his desk. "I write under the name of Ralph Hope and Genson Barak is my Swedish detective."

Amy shook her head, "I haven't come across any of your books. I'll ask Miss White in the public library."

"Here's my latest one," he said, taking a book from the pile. "'A rose by any other name', you keep it. Tell me what you think when you've read it."

"Thank you, I will. See you tomorrow."

Clutching the book and her folder, Amy made her way back down the garden.

Tom Mears was still tending his flowerbed.

"Did you get the job?" he asked, straightening up.

"Yes, I did, and he gave me one of his books," she said waving it.

"Ah, he's a right good writer," Tom said. "But he don't know anything about gardening." He chuckled. "I'm staying on tomorrow to get you settled, so don't you fret. See you then."

As Amy got on her bike, she was conscious of a fierce excitement. She rode quickly away.

Next day, she wheeled her bike up the path and parked it at the side of the tool shed. Old Tom was already there. He showed her where he kept the tools, all clean and neatly arranged in rows. He showed her around the garden, pointing out the marigolds, the geraniums, the roses, all the while giving her tips on how to care for them.

When they came to the bottom of the garden, Tom waved his hand dismissively. "I ain't got time for weeds," he said. "This used to be a lawn in the old days, but the nettles and the brambles crept in, and I gave it no heed. It takes all my time to keep the top garden neat and tidy."

Amy looked around the weed-strewn patch. It had been allowed to go wild. She could see nettles and foxgloves peeping their heads above the long grass. Ivy grew on the trees, flanking the end of the garden and brambles were doing their best to invade.

"This looks quite a challenge, but I think I could do something with it," she said slowly, "I'll have to talk to Mr Jackson."

"Well, good luck to you, lassie," Tom walked off slowly with a wave of his hand.

Amy went up to the house. As she walked up the path, she brushed against a bush of lavender, sending the scent wafting all around her.

Ralph was sitting at his desk in front of the French windows staring into space. His back was turned away, but as she approached, he seemed to sense her presence. He got up, opened the window and beckoned. The heady scent of the lavender followed her in.

"Well, what do you think?" he asked.

"I love your garden, and I can manage it for you," she said, gazing around the room, the shelves of books, the vase of flowers on the side table, the open books scattered everywhere.

"Sit for a minute," he said, waving at the chair facing the desk.

Books were balanced precariously on the chair seat. She lifted them carefully, wondering where to put them.

"On the floor, anywhere," he said looking at her over his glasses.

Amy was too shy to tell him she had spent most of the night reading his book and was startled when he said, "And what did you think of my book?"

"I can't tell you until I've finished it," she said turning her head towards the garden, "but I can tell you something much more important."

She could see from his face that he wasn't used to that sort of answer, so she quickly said, "The book is fine, but the bottom of your garden isn't."

Ralph sat back playing with his pen, a fierce look on his face, "Oh? And what's so important about the bottom of my garden?"

"You've let it go to rack and ruin," she said boldly. "It's got the makings of a wild garden, and I can make it a proper one for you if you want me to."

"Do whatever you think fit," he said, tapping his pen on the desk.

Amy took her courage in both hands, "I doubt if you've seen how awful it is," she said, "Why don't you come and have a look?"

Ralph gave her an impatient look. "My dear young lady, I've got a writing schedule to keep to, I can't go wandering around the garden with you."

"So, what were you doing when you invited me in?" she asked.

Ralph was taken aback. He looked at the slim golden-haired girl in front of him.

"Well, I, er, I've just got Genson trapped in a cellar, and I don't know how to get him out, so I was taking a break."

"Come on then," Amy turned to the door. "A walk is just what you need."

As he stood up, she saw him properly for the first time. He was younger than she'd thought. His smile crinkled around his eyes, and he moved with a rhythmic grace that set her heart pounding.

They went out into the garden and walked down the path to the end. Amy had a strange feeling he wanted to hold her hand and was aware that he kept looking at her. What did he see?

Then, to her surprise, he did hold her hand as they arrived at the overgrown patch.

She gently disengaged her hand without saying anything, but inside, she thought how right it felt. Trying to regain control, she said, "Look at this wilderness. It needs a lot of work, but if you like, I can turn it into a real wild garden."

"It does look a bit of a mess." She could see he was disturbed in some way, but not, she thought by the nettles and the general neglect.

"I hadn't realised Old Tom had let it go like this. Anyway, what's so important about a wild garden?"

Amy looked at him in surprise, "It's very important. Farmers are ripping up hedgerows and using pesticides in the fields. Insects and animals are having a hard time of it. Making a wild garden with lots of flowers with pollen for bees and having a habitat for other insects, birds and small animals can make up for what's happening."

"But I've got flowers in the top garden, why would I want more?"

"If I can get this under control and we sprinkle the right sort of flower seeds on it, not only will the birds, bees and other animals love it, but you will as well."

Ralph looked at her with respect. "Go ahead and ask me for any help you need, and you were right to take me for a walk. I've just thought of how to get Genson out of the cellar." He grinned and turned back to the house.

For the rest of the day, Amy felt as though something special had happened. She worked with a will until it was time to go home. As she was cleaning the tools, she felt a presence. Looking around, she saw that Ralph had come out onto the terrace and was looking in her direction. She closed the shed door, gave him a friendly wave and set off on her bike.

Amy worked hard throughout the year on the formal garden, keeping it in good shape, as well as tending the wild garden, removing the brambles, nettles, thistles and docks that threatened it. Ralph had taken to helping her on occasion as a break from writing. They had sown the flower seeds in the wild garden together and now, as the New Year began to move from spring to summer, flowers were showing up above the grass.

Amy found that she enjoyed Ralph's company while they worked together, and, as a result, their friendship grew.

One sunny summer's day, as they were walking down the path together, Ralph took her hand and squeezed it.

"Your wild garden makes me so happy. I'm glad you came into my life," he said as they reached the bottom of the path. He turned to look at her and Amy felt her heart swell within her.

Can he read my thoughts? I love this man, she thought, *I wonder if he loves me.*

She looked across the waving grass and the multitude of flowers as he took both her hands in his and said, "You must know that my love for you has grown and blossomed like your garden, and I need you with me forever."

Amy looked into his eyes and smiled as he pulled her towards him.

The Happy End Series
Available from Amazon

Book One: The Witch at Happy End
Book Two: More Witchery at Happy End
Book Three: Tales from Barrow Magna
Book Four: More Tales from Barrow Magna

www.ingramcontent.com/pod-product-compliance
Ingram Content Group UK Ltd.
Pitfield, Milton Keynes, MK11 3LW, UK
UKHW022235230426
12048UKWH00018BA/1278